SNOW BORED

Librarian Reviewer

Chris Kreie

Media Specialist, Eden Prairie Schools, MN

MS in Information Media, St. Cloud State University, MN

Reading Consultant

Elizabeth Stedem

Educator/Consultant, Colorado Springs, CO

MA in Elementary Education, University of Denver, CO

First published in the United States in 2007
by Stone Arch Books,
151 Good Counsel Drive, P.O. Box 669,
Mankato, Minnesota 56002.
www.stonearchbooks.com

First published by Evans Brothers Ltd,
2A Portman Mansions, Chiltern Street,
London W1U 6NR, United Kingdom.

Library of Congress Cataloging-in-Publication Data
Lawrie, Robin.
    Snow Bored / by Robin and Chris Lawrie; illustrated by Robin
Lawrie.
        p. cm. — (Ridge Riders)
    Summary: Bored when their practice hill gets buried in snow, Slam
and his friends try snowboarding instead and blame Fiona for everything
that goes wrong, but when Slam tries to make up with her by bringing a set
of the bicycle snow tires his father devised, things go from bad to worse.
    ISBN-13: 978-1-59889-349-6 (library binding)
    ISBN-10: 1-59889-349-1 (library binding)
    ISBN-13: 978-1-59889-444-8 (paperback)
    ISBN-10: 1-59889-444-7 (paperback)
    [1. Snowboarding—Fiction. 2. All terrain cycling—Fiction.
3. Bicycle racing—Fiction.] I. Lawrie, Chris. II. Title.
PZ7.L438218Sno 2007
[Fic]—dc22   2006026634

1 2 3 4 5 6 12 11 10 09 08 07

Printed in the United States of America

SNOW BORED

by Robin and Chris Lawrie
illustrated by Robin Lawrie

STONE ARCH BOOKS
MINNEAPOLIS   SAN DIEGO

The Ridge Riders

 Hi, my name is "Slam" Duncan.

This is Aziz. We call him Dozy.

Then there's Larry.

This is Fiona.

And Andy.

I'm Andy. (Andy is deaf. He uses sign language instead of talking.)

We all love mountain biking on Westridge hill!

Except . . .

when it . . .

snows!

We were in training for the "Sword in the Stump" series of mountain bike races. But it had been snowing for days and we were bored silly, because our practice hill was covered with snow.

> AT LEAST WE DON'T HAVE TO GO TO SCHOOL!

Then Dozy had a bright idea.
He borrowed a pair of his big brother's old sneakers.

He took out the laces and cut off the backs.
Next, he took the wheels off an old skateboard.
He nailed on the sneakers.

He had made a . . .

SNOWBOARD!

Soon everyone was doing it, creating a huge demand for old sneakers and skateboards.

In fact, some not so old sneakers and skateboards got borrowed, too.

So, where was I? With everyone else!

9

We built some mega jumps
and were getting huge air.

OOOOHH!

Then "Punk"
Tuer showed up.
He had a real snowboard
from his dad's store and made
our tricks look awful!

Fiona hadn't been able to join in the fun because she had been helping with the work at her dad's farm. Now she showed up with a pair of skis. She got the biggest air ever!

It was crazy! We measured one of her jumps from take-off to landing. We could not believe it. It was amazing.

200 feet!

Things were getting out of hand.

Soon the accidents started to happen.
A major crash sent Larry to the
hospital with a sprained wrist
and a concussion.
For a while he forgot his
name, but they let him
out anyway.

Dozy hit the jump at a
funny angle, flipped, and
broke his board.

AARGHH!

Andy had a bad take-off and
landed in a tree. He never did
find his board.

Punk's expensive new
snowboard got broken
in two.
As usual, he looked
around for someone
to blame.

Poor Fiona! Why did they have to blame her?

You've ruined our jump with your stupid skis. Why don't you go back to your farm!

Yeah, my board is broken because of your girly skis!

And Larry got a concussion because of you and your skis!

Hang on, I am Larry!

And then, of course, my sister wanted her sneakers back.

That's it! I've had just about enough of this!

Fiona went back to her farm. The rest of us had nothing to do but hang out at my dad's garage. Soon, he was sick of that.

Okay. Bring me some old bike tires and I'll try something.

So we did. Dad drilled about twenty holes in each tire.

What's he doing?

BZZIP! BZZIP!

BOLTS   NUTS

What do you think, Einstein?

Then he fit little bolts to each hole, and made four sets of . . .

SNOW TIRES!

We put them on our bikes and went to
Westridge for some training.

The new tires worked really well in the snow.
But I started to feel bad about Fiona. We had
been really horrible to her. So I made her a
set of studded tires and rode up to her farm
with them.

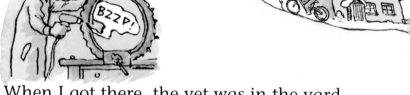

When I got there, the vet was in the yard,
talking to Fiona's mom.

They're out there, you know. Every day
there are new sightings. Lights in the sky,
strange messages on the radio . . .

He had been working too hard.

Farm work, plus a heavy snowfall, meant that the poor man hadn't slept in days, and he'd started seeing things.

I went in the house to talk to Fiona.

Fiona was busy!
Weak or orphaned lambs need special care, and this was Fiona's job. With all the snow, there were lots of them!

I offered her the tires, but she said:

No thanks, Slam. I've got twenty-four lambs to feed, and I also have to exercise Baggage.

She's stuck inside in this weather, so I have to ride her every day.

Little people with green skin!

The vet was still talking about aliens. I was afraid he would start telling me about them next, so I headed for the hill.

The tires were great, but there
was one problem.

Then Fiona turned to go.

A pheasant suddenly rushed into the air from under a bush. Baggage took off like a rocket.

I was afraid Fiona
was going to fall
off, so I went
after her.

I caught up with them in Fiona's yard,
Baggage slipped and had a terrible fall.

They both lay still in the snow for what
seemed like years.

At last, Fiona got up, and after a while, so
did Baggage.

It didn't look good.

We led her into the stable, where she lay
down again.

> It's no good, Slam, my parents are out. We'll
> have to call the vet. I think she's
> hurt herself.

The girl at the vet's said:

> He's at Miss White's farm. Try
> his cell phone.

But it was turned off.
I was going to have to
look for him.

It was snowing hard again, and by now
it was dark. So I turned on my lights.

Be careful, Slam.

I headed
for the road
that led to Miss
White's farm. I was just in time to see the
vet's car reach the turn and start heading
back to town.

I had to catch him.

It was the scariest ride of my life.

I was
flashing my lights
on and off and shouting at
him. But he just went faster.
We got to a stop sign.
He slammed on his brakes.
I slammed on mine.
His were better.

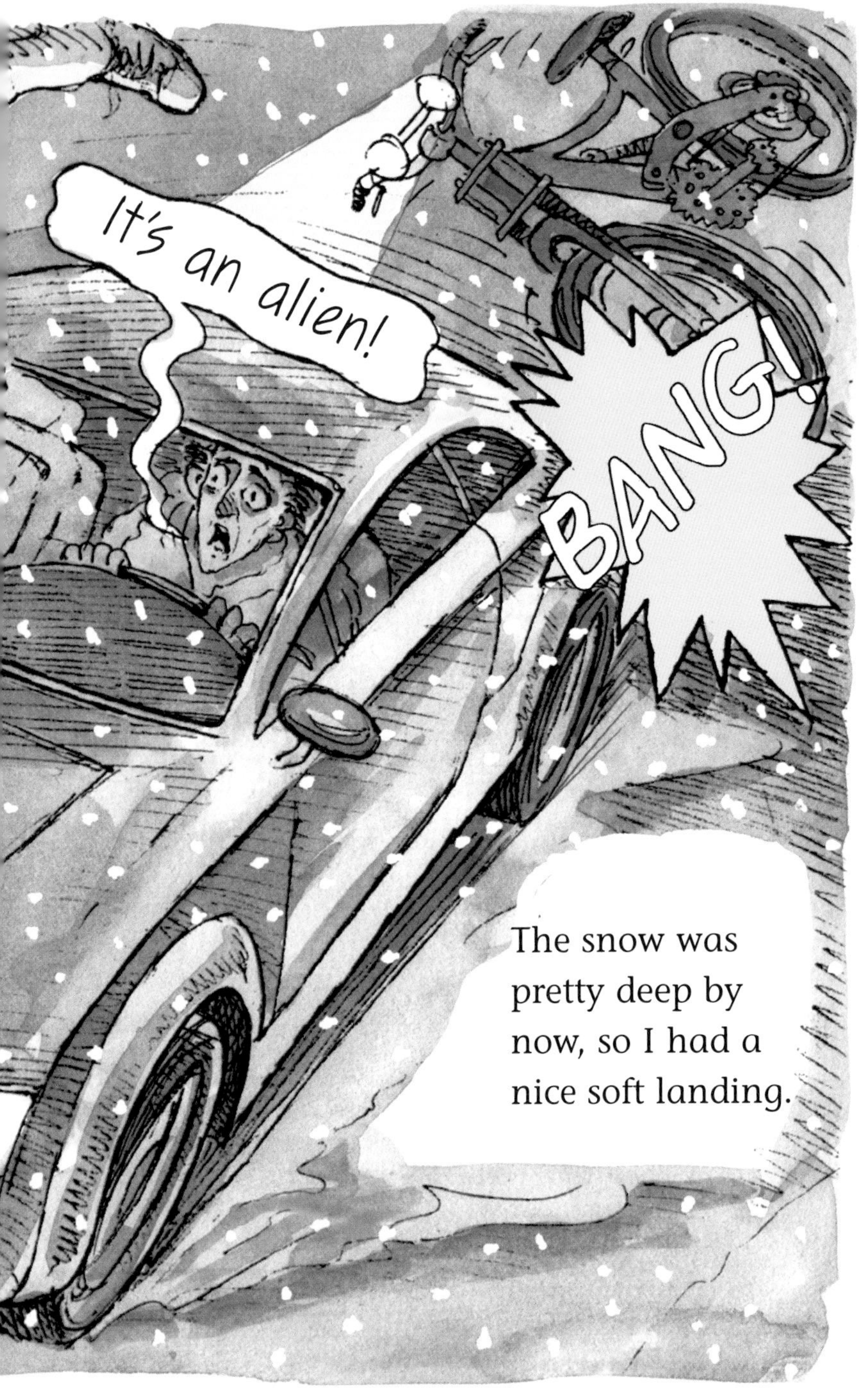

The snow was pretty deep by now, so I had a nice soft landing.

It took a little while to calm him down.

Back at Fiona's house, the vet took a look at Baggage.

We offered him some cocoa, and soon . . .

About the Author and Illustrator

Robin and Chris Lawrie wrote the *Ridge Riders* books together, and Robin illustrated them. Their inspiration for these books is their son. They wanted to write books that he would find interesting. Many of the *Ridge Riders* books are based on adventures he and his friends had while biking.

Robin and Chris live in England, and will soon be moving to a big, old house that is also home to sixty bats.

Glossary

alien (AY-lee-uhn)—a creature from another planet

banned (BAND)—forbidden to enter

bolt (BOHLT)—a strong metal pin used with a metal nut to hold things together

deaf (DEF)—not being able to hear well or to hear at all

rangers (RAYN-jurz)—people in charge of a forest or park

studded (STUD-id)—something studded is decorated with pieces of metal

surface (SUR-fiss)—the outer layer

traction (TRAK-shuhn)—the power that keeps something from slipping on a surface

veterinarian or **vet** (vet-ur-uh-NER-ee-uhn)—a doctor for animals

Internet Sites

Do you want to know more about subjects related to this book? Or are you interested in learning about other topics? Then check out FactHound, a fun, easy way to find Internet sites.

Our investigative staff has already sniffed out great sites for you!

Here's how to use FactHound:

1. Visit *www.facthound.com*

2. Select your grade level.

3. To learn more about subjects related to this book, type in the book's ISBN number: **1598893491**.

4. Click the **Fetch It** button.

FactHound will fetch the best Internet sites for you!

Discussion Questions

1. What do you think about the way the boys treated Fiona? Was it fair of them? Why were they upset with her?

2. Why does the veterinarian think that aliens have landed?

3. The Ridge Riders's plans for biking are ruined by the snow. They decide to build snowboards. What are some other things they could have done? What do you do when weather ruins your plans?

Writing Prompts

1. Do you believe in aliens? Write a story in which aliens land in your neighborhood. Don't forget to describe the aliens!

2. The Ridge Riders build snowboards out of skateboards and sneakers. Create an invention of your own. What is it built out of? What would it do? Draw a picture of it and label the parts.

Read other adventures of the Ridge Riders

Cheat Challenge

Slam Duncan and his friends, the Ridge Riders, don't know what to think when they come across a sword buried deep in their mountain-biking course. It's part of a new racing course contest called Excalibur. Then Slam accidentally gets a look at the map of the course, but he knows he can't tell his teammates the map's secrets.

Fear 3.1

While rock climbing, Slam loses his foothold. Luckily, his safety harness holds, but that doesn't stop Slam from being terrified. Soon, he can't even manage to complete the mountain biking courses he's ridden on for years. Will Slam ever get over this phobia for good?

White Lightning

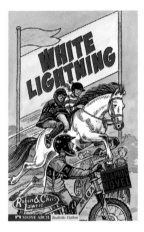

Someone smashed the Ridge Riders' practice jumps, and they suspect Fiona and her horse-riding friends. The boys are so mean to Fiona that she leaves. Then Slam gets a flat tire and has to race back home to get his spare, and he only has 50 minutes! Now a horse would come in handy!

Radar Riders

The Ridge Riders need a new place to race, so they build a wild new course. It takes all their skills, and some techno-wizardry, to keep them on track before they run into some unexpected turns.

Check out Stone Arch Books adventure novels!

Blackbeard's Sword
The Pirate King of the Carolinas

Blackbeard holds the Carolinas in a grip of terror. Lieutenant Maynard and his men of the Royal Navy are after the pirate. They enlist the aid of young Jacob Webster and his father, but Maynard doesn't know that Jacob thinks Blackbeard is a hero!

Hot Iron
The Adventures of a Civil War Powder Boy

Twelve-year-old Charlie O'Leary signs aboard the USS Varuna as it steams its way toward the mouth of the Mississippi River to fight the Confederate Navy. Will his ship survive the awesome Battle of New Orleans?